"Turn my eyes away from worthless things"
—Psalm 119:37

ZONDERKIDZ

The Berenstain Bears® Bear Family Treasury
Copyright © 2010 by Berenstain Publishing, Inc.
Illustrations © 2010 by Berenstain Publishing, Inc.

Requests for information should be addressed to:

Zondervan, 3900 Sparks Dr., Grand Rapids, Michigan 49546

ISBN 978-0-310-62156-0 (hardcover)

Trouble With Things ISBN 9780310720911   Copyright © 2012 by Berenstain Publishing, Inc.
Gossip Gang ISBN 9780310720850   Copyright © 2011 by Berenstain Publishing, Inc.
Show Some Respect ISBN 9780310720867   Copyright © 2011 by Berenstain Publishing, Inc.
Kindness Counts ISBN 9780310712572   Copyright © 2010 by Berenstain Publishing, Inc.
God Loves You! ISBN 9780310712503   Copyright © 2008 by Berenstain Publishing, Inc.
Faithful Friends ISBN 9780310712534   Copyright © 2009 by Berenstain Publishing, Inc.
A Job Well Done ISBN 9780310712541   Copyright © 2010 by Berenstain Publishing, Inc.
The Gift of Courage ISBN 9780310712565   Copyright © 2010 by Berenstain Publishing, Inc.

14 15 16 17 18 19 • 12 11 10 9 8 7 6 5 4 3 2 1

The Berenstain Bears

Living Lights™

Bear Family Treasury

written by
Jan & Mike Berenstain

The Berenstain Bears

and the

Trouble with THINGS

written by
Jan & Mike Berenstain

Living Lights

ZONDERkidz

Like most cubs their age, Brother and Sister had a lot of things—things like toys, games, books, puzzles, bikes, skates, soccer balls, a deluxe swing set, a super-bounce trampoline, seventeen Bearbie dolls, the complete Space Grizzlies video library, and much, much more.

But, even though they had all these things, there were plenty of others they would like to have too.

One morning, Brother and Sister noticed Mama getting ready to go out.

"Where are you going, Mama?" Sister asked.

"To the Bear Country Mall," said Mama. "We need new sheets and pillowcases. Our old ones are almost worn out."

"Can we come?" Brother and Sister asked. "There are lots of things we need at the mall too."

"Well ..." said Mama. She wasn't so sure there was anything the cubs really needed. They already had so much. But Papa chimed in as well.

"Let's all go," he said. "I'd like to look at some new fishing gear."

Mama wasn't so sure that Papa really needed new fishing gear, either. But they collected Honey and piled into the car for a trip to the mall.

The Bear Country Mall was humongous. It looked like a giant castle with towers and flags flying. And its parking lot was humongous, too.

The Bear family had to park far away
and take a long hike to the entrance.

Inside the mall, they joined huge crowds of bears
all busily shopping for *things*.

First, they stopped at a store for the sheets and pillowcases
that Mama needed. Brother and Sister were bored.
"Can we go to the toy store?" they asked.
"We'll see," said Mama.

Next, they went to a store for the fishing gear that Papa wanted.
He looked greedily at all the shiny rods, reels, and lures.

He bought himself a new
salmon reel. Brother and
Sister were still bored.

"Can we go to the toy store now?"
they asked.
"We'll see," said Papa.

As they walked through the mall, they passed near the toy store.

"Look!" said Brother and Sister. "We see the toy store! Can we go in? Please? Please? Pretty please?"

Papa and Mama looked at each other and shrugged.
"Well, why not?" they said.
Mama and Papa quickly found out why not.

As soon as they were inside the toy store, Brother and Sister began to ask for things, all kinds of things. Brother asked for a Space Grizzlies play set.

Sister asked for a pink Bearbie dream house with matching pink sports car and pink swimming pool.

And they both asked for new skateboards, new video games, new puzzles, new craft kits, new rollerblades, new minibikes, new baseball gloves, new hockey sticks, and anything else they could think of.

Mama and Papa Bear were not pleased.

"I am shocked ... shocked by how greedy you are!" said Papa, holding his new fishing reel behind his back.

"Well," Mama said in his ear, "maybe we shouldn't be so shocked. After all, we're the ones who gave them all their things to begin with."

"Hmmm," said Papa.
"I guess you're right.
What should we do?"

"I have an idea,"
said Mama. "Let's
stop by the mall's
bookstore."

In the bookstore, Mama picked out a book.

"This is just what we need," she said, opening it. It was a storybook Bible.

She showed the cubs a picture of a king wearing a golden crown and rich robes. He was seated in a garden. All around were beautiful flowers. The colors of the flowers were even brighter than the king's crown and robes.

"Who's that guy?" asked Brother.
"That's King Solomon," said Mama.
"Now listen."

She read:

"See how the flowers of the field grow. They do not labor or spin. Yet I tell you that not even Solomon in all his splendor was dressed like one of these."

"Huh?" said Sister.
"What's that mean?" asked Brother.

"It means," explained Papa, "nothing that a king with all his money can buy is as beautiful as the simple flowers God creates."

"Oh," said Brother and Sister, thinking that over.

"Well," said Mama, "it's time we were getting home."

Soon, they were driving through the
beautiful spring countryside.
"Stop!" said Sister.
"What's the matter?" asked Mama.
"Look at all the flowers," said Sister.

They were passing through
a field of bright yellow flowers.
"Can we stop to pick some?"
Sister asked.

The whole family gathered big armfuls of lovely, fragrant wildflowers. Sister sniffed them deeply.

"I guess these flowers really are more beautiful than King Solly-Man in all his splendor," she said.

"That's 'King Solomon,' dear," said Mama. "But you are right. The things God gives us are much better than anything we can buy."

"What sort of things?" asked Brother.

"Things like the warm sun in the day and the bright moon and twinkling stars at night," said Papa.

"Things like the fresh air we breathe and the cool water we drink," added Mama.

"What about the birds in the sky and the fish in the sea?" asked Sister.

"And clouds and rainbows and rain and snow!" put in Brother.

"Snow!" yelled Honey. "Well, not today, Honey," laughed Papa.

The Bear family got back in their car and drove on. As they came to the top of the hill, they could see their tree house home in the valley below, lit up by the golden sunset.

"But one of the best things of all, in God's whole wide world," said Papa, "is our own home, sweet tree."

"And," added Mama, "our own sweet family
to go inside."

The Berenstain Bears'
Gossip Gang

written by
Jan & Mike Berenstain

Living Lights™

ZONDERkidz

Lizzy and Suzie were Sister Bear's best friends. They liked doing all sorts of things together. They rode bikes and jumped rope.

They played soccer outside and video games inside. They had tea parties with their dolls and stuffed animals. And sometimes they just sat around and talked.

They talked about anything and everything. They talked about TV shows and toys, about games and songs, about pets, parents, brothers and sisters, and, of course, their other friends.

"Did you hear about Queenie?" asked Lizzy. Queenie McBear was an older cub who was very popular. "I heard she has a big crush on Too-Tall Grizzly, but he has a crush on Bonnie Brown!"

"Oooh!" said the others. They were too young to have crushes yet. But they liked to talk about them.

"Did you get a load of that new cub in school?" asked Suzie. "His name is actually Teddy Bear!" The others laughed. Suzie had been a new cub not so long ago. But she didn't seem to remember.

"Well, I saw Anna Bruin the other day," said Sister, "and, you know, I think she put on some weight. She looks sort of chubby."

Lizzy and Suzie giggled.

The three friends talked for a while longer but it was soon dinnertime. "See you!" said Sister, heading home. She liked talking to Lizzy and Suzie about other cubs. It made her feel special and "in-the-know."

Back home, Mama and Papa were setting the table. Brother and Sister joined them.

"Do you know what Herb the mailman told me?" Papa said to Mama as he laid the silverware.

"I can't imagine," said Mama, busy putting out plates.

"He said someone saw Mayor Honeypot throwing a banana peel out his car window. Imagine—the mayor, himself, a litterbug!"

"Now, Papa," said Mama, "you know that's just gossip. You shouldn't spread stories like that."

Papa looked a little ashamed. "I guess you're right. It was just so interesting."

As they sat down to dinner, Sister had a question.

"Mama," she asked, "what's gossip?"

"Well," Mama began, "gossip is when we tell stories about others—especially stories that make them look bad. It's something we do to make ourselves feel special. It can be very hurtful.

"As the Bible says, 'gossip separates close friends.'"

"Oh," said Sister, worried. She thought maybe saying that Anna looked sort of chubby was gossip. She decided not to think about it anymore.

The next day, Sister saw Lizzy and Suzie walking ahead of her on the way to the playground. They were busy talking and didn't notice Sister coming up behind them. As Sister drew near, she overheard them talking ... about her!

"Do you know what Anna told me about Sister?" began Lizzy.

"No, what?" asked Suzie, eagerly.

"She saw Sister's spelling quiz when Teacher Jane was handing back the papers, and it was marked, '60%—very poor!'" said Lizzy.

"Wow!" said Suzie.

When Sister heard that, she stopped short. In the first place, it wasn't true. Her quiz was marked "70%—fair." That wasn't too good, but it wasn't as bad as all that.

And, in the second place, why were Lizzy and Suzie gossiping about her? They were supposed to be her best friends. She felt so bad she hid behind a tree until Lizzy and Suzie were out of sight.

As Sister came out from behind the tree, Brother Bear walked by. He was on his way to play catch with Cousin Fred.

"What on earth …?" he said. "Why are you hiding behind a tree?"

"I didn't want Lizzy and Suzie to see me," said Sister.

"Why not?" he asked.

"Because they were gossiping about me and I heard," said Sister. "I was so embarrassed!"

"I'm sorry," said Brother. "Why don't you come along with me and play catch with Fred?"
So they did.

At the playground, they started tossing the ball around. Sister could see Lizzy and Suzie on the swings, nearby. They waved and Sister waved back. Then she got angry.

"You know what I heard about Lizzy?" she called, loudly, to Fred.
"I heard that she is a big silly dope!"

"Huh?" said Fred.

"And you know what I heard about Suzie?" she yelled, even louder. "I heard that she is a funny-faced noodle-brain!"

"Sister!" said Brother.

When Lizzy and Suzie overheard Sister, they jumped off the swings and came charging over.

"Why are you saying bad things about us?" they yelled. "We thought you were our best friend!"

"That's just what I thought!" said Sister. "But I heard you gossiping about me on the way here!"

"Oh," said Lizzy. She hadn't thought about it that way. "I guess you're right. We were gossiping about you. I'm sorry!"

"Me too!" said Suzie.

Sister got over being angry right away. After all, Lizzy and Suzie were her best friends.

"That's okay," she said. "Maybe it would be better if we just didn't gossip about anyone."

Lizzy and Suzie agreed. Gossip clearly was more trouble than it was worth.

"As it says in the Bible," said Fred, who liked to memorize things, "'The tongue also is a fire.'"

"What's that supposed to mean?" said Sister.

"Just that gossiping is like playing with fire," said Fred. "You can get burnt."

"I think a game of baseball would be a lot more fun than gossip," said Brother.

"Yeah," said Sister. "Let's play!"

"I'll bet me and Fred can beat the three of you, put together," said Brother.

"You're on!" said Sister.
"Play ball!" called Fred.

Sister and her friends won.
After all, it was three against two.

The Berenstain Bears®

Show Some Respect

written by
Jan and Mike Berenstain

Living Lights™

ZONDERkidz

It was a beautiful summer morning and the Bear family was going on a picnic. Mama and Papa packed up the picnic things. Brother, Sister, and Honey were very excited. Grizzly Gramps and Gran were coming too.

"I made a pot of my special wilderness stew for the picnic," said Gran.
"Mmm-mmm!" said Gramps. "Wilderness stew—my favorite!"
"Yuck-o!" muttered Brother. "Wilderness stew—not one of my favorites."

Sister laughed.

"What was that, Brother?" asked Mama.

"Oh, nothing, Mama," said Brother. "Come on, Sis. Let's pick out a good picnic spot."

The family headed down the sunny dirt road
to find the perfect spot for their picnic. Sister and
Brother ran on ahead.

"Wait for us please, cubs," said Mama. But Sister
and Brother paid no attention.

"Hmmm ...," said Mama, none too pleased.

"I remember a good picnic spot right in these trees," said Papa. "We used to come here when I was in school."

"That was about a hundred years ago," said Sister.
"It's pretty run down now. Let's find a better spot."
"Hmmm!" said Papa, none too pleased.

"I know a lovely spot down by that pond," said Mama. "Papa and I came here on our first date."

"That was an awful long time ago,"
said Brother. "It's full of mosquitoes
now. Let's find a better spot."
"Hmmm!" said Mama and Papa,
none too pleased.

"I recall a time when Gramps and I had a nice picnic on top of Big Bear Hill," said Gran as they went on their way. "There was a lovely view, and …"

"Now, Gran," interrupted Mama. "We don't want to climb all the way up Big Bear Hill. Let's find a better spot."

"Hmmm!" said Gran, none too pleased.

The Bear family trudged across the countryside. They were getting hungry, hot, and tired.

"I have a good idea for a picnic spot," said Gramps. "How about we all …"

"Now, Gramps," interrupted Papa. "We don't need any help—we know what we're doing."

Gramps stopped short.

"Now, just a doggone minute!" he said. "It seems to me that you folks aren't showing much respect for your elders."

"That's right," agreed Gran. "Brother and Sister are being disrespectful to Mama and Papa."

"And Mama and Papa are being disrespectful to you and me," added Gramps. "You know, us old folks know a thing or two. As the Bible says, 'Age should speak; advanced years should teach wisdom.'"

"But, Gramps!" said Papa.

"But me no 'buts,' sonny!" said Gramps. "'A wise son heeds his father's instruction,'" he added, quoting the Bible, again.

"Sonny?" said Brother and Sister. It never occurred to them that
Papa was someone's "sonny."

When they thought it over, Brother, Sister, Mama, and Papa realized that Gramps and Gran were right. They were being disrespectful.

"We're sorry!" said Brother and Sister. "We were excited about the picnic and forgot our manners. We'll be sure to show more respect from now on."

"And we're sorry too!" said Mama and Papa. "We know we shouldn't speak to our elders that way."

"That's fine," smiled Gran. "All is forgiven. Now come along. Gramps will pick a good picnic-spot for us. He's Bear Country's foremost picnic-spot picker-outer."

"Yes, indeedy," said Gramps. "Besides, if we leave it up to all of you, we might starve!"

"Where are we going, Gramps?" asked Brother
and Sister as Gramps led them across the countryside.
    "Never fear," said Gramps. "Grizzly Gramps, the
picnic-spot picker-outer, is here!"

They marched over hill and dale, through wood and field.
"Now there's the perfect picnic spot!" said Gramps, at last.
"But, Gramps!" said Sister. "That's your own house."

"That's right, young'un," he smiled. "Didn't you ever hear of a backyard picnic?"

Gramps and Papa got the grill fired up and they added honey grilled salmon to Gran's wilderness stew.

"Mmm-mmm!" said Brother and Sister. "Honey grilled salmon—that's our favorite!"

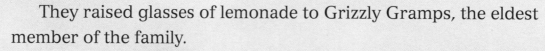

They raised glasses of lemonade to Grizzly Gramps, the eldest member of the family.

"To Grizzly Gramps," said Papa, "Bear Country's best picnic-spot picker-outer!"

"You know," said Gramps, as he dug into a big helping of wilderness stew, "it's about time I got a little respect around here."

The Berenstain Bears®
Kindness Counts

written by Jan and Mike Berenstain

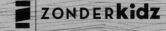

Living Lights™

ZONDERkidz

Brother Bear was a bear of many interests. He enjoyed sports such as baseball, soccer, football, and basketball. He liked to draw and paint, and he was interested in science. He had hobbies like collecting stamps and baseball cards, and he enjoyed fishing and playing video games. But the thing he enjoyed most of all was building model airplanes.

He started building models with Papa when he was very young.
At first, they made simple plastic models. But, soon, they were
creating flying models out of lightweight wood and paper. Before
long, Brother could build models all by himself.

He kept building bigger and better models that could fly longer, farther, and higher. On trips to the park with Sister Bear, he always took along his latest model for flight trials. It was a thrill to wind its propeller for the first time, let it go, and watch it fly across the park.

One Saturday afternoon, Brother tried out his latest creation, a big model plane painted bright red called *The Meteor*. He set it down on the grass and wound the propeller. Sister joined some of her friends nearby. One of them was minding her younger brother, Billy. He was playing with a small model plane like the ones Brother had when he was little.

When Billy saw Brother's big new plane, he came over to take a look.

"Wow!" he said. "That's beautiful!"

"Thanks! She's called *The Meteor*. I built her myself," Brother said proudly.

"Wow!" said Billy. "I wish I could build a plane like that."

Brother finished winding the propeller and picked up *The Meteor*.
"Can I help you fly it?" asked Billy.

Brother was proud of his models and careful with them too. They took a long time to build and were easy to break. If you didn't launch them just right, they could take a nosedive and crash.

"Well," said Brother doubtfully, "I don't know...," But he remembered how Papa always let him help out when they were building and flying model planes. That's how he learned—by helping Papa.

"Well," said Brother, "okay. You can help me hold it."

"Oh, boy! Thanks!" said Billy.

Brother knelt down and let Billy hold the model with him.

"Now, remember," said Brother, "don't throw it—let it fly out of your hands. Here we go—one, two, three ... *fly*!"

They both let go, and the big red *Meteor* lifted up and away, its propeller whirring.

"YIPEEE!" yelled Billy. "Look at it fly!"

But Brother was worried. *The Meteor* was climbing up too steeply. As they watched, *The Meteor* rose high above the park. It seemed to pause in midair. Its nose suddenly dipped down, and it went into a dive. *The Meteor* hit the ground with a nasty *crunch*!

Brother and Billy ran to the wrecked model. Brother sadly picked it up and looked at the damage. Billy's big sister and the others noticed the excitement and came over.

"Oh, no!" said Billy. "Is it my fault? Did I do something wrong? Did I throw it instead of letting it fly like you said?"

Brother shook his head. "Of course not!" he said. "You did fine. This is my fault. I didn't get the balance right. It's tail heavy. That's why it went up too steep, paused, and dove down. That's called 'stalling.'"

"Are you going to fix it?" asked Billy.

"Sure!" laughed Brother. "'Build 'em, fly 'em, crash 'em, fix 'em!' That's my motto."

"Could I help you?" wondered Billy.

"Now, Billy," said his big sister, "you're too young to help."

But Brother remembered how Papa always used to let him help. That was how he learned about model airplanes.

"That's okay," Brother told Billy's big sister. "I don't mind. I could use a little help."

So Billy came along to the Bears' tree house. Mama and Papa were pleased that Brother was being so kind to young Billy.

"It's just as the Good Book says," Mama said, "'Blessed are the merciful, for they will be shown mercy.'"

"Yes," agreed Papa, "and it also says in the Bible that a kind person benefits himself."

"What does that mean?" wondered Brother.

"It means that no act of kindness is wasted," said Papa. "Any kindness you do will always come back to you."

Blessed are the merciful, for they will be shown mercy.
Matthew 5:7

Every afternoon that week, Billy helped Brother work on the plane. He didn't know very much, but he learned a lot and he had lots of fun. Brother had fun too. He enjoyed teaching, and he liked having a helper who looked up to him.

The next Saturday, *The Meteor* was ready for another flight. Brother and Billy took it down to the park. Everyone came along to watch. They wound *The Meteor's* propeller, held it up, and let it fly. It lifted away and rose in a long, even curve.

"This looks like a good flight!" said Brother.

The *Meteor* flew on and on across the field. Slowly, it came down, landing clear on the other side of the park in a three-point landing. Brother and Billy ran over. It was in perfect shape.

"Hurray!" yelled Billy, jumping up and down.

Brother began to wind up the propeller for another try, but he noticed a group of older cubs coming into the park. They carried a lot of interesting equipment and wore jackets that said "Bear Country Rocket Club." Brother went over to watch. They were setting up a model rocket. They were going to fire it off and let it come down by parachute. Brother was excited.

"Excuse me," he said to the cub in charge, "do you think I could help you launch the rocket?"

The cub shook his head. "Sorry!" he said. "You're too young. It's too dangerous."

Brother walked away sadly. But he noticed that Billy was staying behind. He was talking to the older cub in charge. The older cub called Brother back.

"My cousin, Billy, tells me you let him help with your model plane," said the older cub. Brother just nodded. The older cub smiled. "That was cool. You seem to know a lot about flying and models. I guess you can help out."

So the rocket club
let Brother hold things
for them, carry things for
them, and squirt a little
glue here and there. He
learned a lot and he was
happy. When it was time
to fire off the rocket, they
even let Brother push
the button.

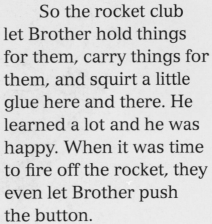

"10, 9, 8, 7, 6, 5, 4, 3, 2, 1 ... *fire!*"
said the cub in charge, and Brother
pushed the button.

There was a loud *WHOOOSH!*

The rocket shot up, leaving a trail of smoke.

High above the park a yellow parachute popped open, and the rocket drifted back to earth.

They ran over to it. It was all twisted and scorched.

"Are you going to fix it?" asked Brother.

"Sure," laughed the older cub. "'Build 'em, fly 'em, crash 'em, fix 'em!' That's our motto."

"Could I help you?" asked Brother.

The older cub thought it over. "Sure," he said, slapping Brother on the back. "Why not?"

So, because Brother Bear had shown a little kindness to someone younger than himself, he became the youngest member, ever, of the Bear Country Rocket Club.

And was he ever proud!

The Berenstain Bears®

God Loves You!

by Stan and Jan Berenstain
with Mike Berenstain

Living Lights™

ZONDERkidz

The first week of school was a busy time for Brother and Sister Bear. It was a time to see old friends, meet new teachers, get their first homework assignments, and sign up for after-school activities.

Sister decided to try out for the big school show. This year it was *The Music Bear*. Sister thought she would be perfect in a leading role. She liked to sing "I Feel Pretty" from *Bearside Story* at home. Mama and Papa always said she was very good.

But there would be a lot of other girls trying out for the show too. Babs Bruno had a very fine voice, and there was Queenie McBear, of course. She thought she was the best singer in the school, and all her friends agreed with her.

THE
MUSIC BEAR
Tryouts

Sister

Brother Bear was trying out too, but not for the school show. He wanted to be on the school basketball team. He was pretty sure he could make it. He had been practicing dribbling and layups in the driveway at home. He played 21 with Papa after supper and always beat him.

Basketball Tryouts

Brother Be

The tryouts for the school play and basketball team were on the same day. After school, Brother went down to the gym and got into a basketball uniform. He and the other boys charged out onto the court and started warming up.

Sister joined a long line of cubs in the
auditorium. Teacher Jane called them up on
the stage one by one to sing a song. Babs
sang "Memory," and she was very good. But
Queenie made a mess of "Tomorrow"! She had
a hard time hitting all the high notes. In spite of
that, all her friends clapped and cheered, and
Queenie took a few bows. Sister glanced over
at Teacher Jane. She didn't look too impressed.

When it was Sister's turn, she sang "I Feel
Pretty" just like she did at home for Mama
and Papa.

In the gym, Brother was puffing and panting away, trying hard to look good. One after another, the boys dribbled, passed, shot layups, and took foul shots while Coach Grizzmeyer looked on and checked off names on a clipboard. You couldn't tell anything by watching him. His face never changed—never a smile, never a frown, not even a wink. The cubs called him Old Stoneface.

Finally, he said, "Okay, men! That's enough! The roster will be posted on the bulletin board outside my office tomorrow."

On his way back to the locker room, Brother couldn't resist stopping to ask, "Coach, do you think I have a shot at making the team?"

Coach Grizzmeyer just shrugged and said, "We'll see, son."

In the auditorium, the auditions for the school show were winding up. Teacher Jane smiled a lot more than Coach Grizzmeyer, but she wasn't giving anything away, either.

"That's all for today, everyone!" she said. "I'll post my choices for the entire cast tomorrow on the bulletin board outside my room."

As Sister left, she couldn't resist stopping to ask, "Teacher Jane, do you think I have a chance of getting one of the main parts?"

But Teacher Jane just smiled and said, "We'll see, my dear."

Sister joined up with Brother as he walked home from school.

"Well, how do you think it went?" asked Sister. "Do you think you made the team?"

"Yeah, I think so!" said Brother hopefully. He really felt he had done well. He knew he was still a little short to be playing on the school team. But he hoped his skills and his hustle would make up for that.

"What about you?" Brother asked. "How did the auditions go?"

"Great, I think," said Sister.

"What did Teacher Jane think?" Brother asked.

"I don't know," said Sister thoughtfully. "She didn't say anything. She just smiled at everybody."

"At least she smiled. Old Stoneface never smiles!"

Sister laughed as they reached their tree house and climbed the steps.

"Oh, well!" she said, shrugging. "We'll find out how we did tomorrow."

And they did ...

The next morning, both Brother and Sister rushed downstairs, gobbled their breakfasts, waved a quick good-bye to Mama and Papa, and got to school faster than they ever had before. They couldn't wait to see how they had done.

Brother rushed to Coach Grizzmeyer's office while Sister scurried to Teacher Jane's room. There were crowds of cubs gathered around the bulletin boards. Brother and Sister struggled to get up close.

Basketball
TEAM
LINEUP

Barry Bruin
Cousin Fred
Too-Tall Grizzly
Bob Bruno
Vinnie Bearkin
Chuck Ursullini
Sam Honeytree
Ralph O'Grizz
Lou Bearens

Chuck
Sam Honey
Ralph O'Griz
Lou Bearens
Brother Bear: Team Manager

Brother glanced quickly down the list of names. There was his, right at the bottom. At first, he felt a rush of relief. But then, he noticed what it said next to his name: Team Manager.

Team manager! TEAM MANAGER? The team manager just picked up basketballs and made sure everybody got on the bus on time. That's not what he wanted to do! He wanted to play; he wanted to shoot and dribble and dunk. He wanted to be a big star!

Crushed, he slunk down the hallway to his classroom.

THE MUSIC BEAR CAST

Ferdy Factual: Henry Hill
Babs Bruno: Marian
Ziggy Grizowsky: The Mayor
Queenie McBear: Mrs. Paroo
Harry Bearkis: Eddie
Bonnie Brown: Eulalie
Anna Grizzle: Gracie
Ron Ursowitz: Mr. Washburn
Sister Bear: Stage Manager

Outside Teacher Jane's room, Sister quickly looked over the cast. At first, she didn't see her name at all. Then she spotted it, right at the bottom.

Sister Bear: Stage Manager.

Stage manager! STAGE MANAGER? All the stage manager did was put away the props and make sure everybody got onstage on time. She didn't want to be stage manager. She wanted to act; she wanted to sing and dance and take bows. She wanted to be a big star!

Miserably, Sister trudged down the hall to her classroom.

When school let out that
afternoon, Brother and Sister
were both feeling very sorry for
themselves. Even the weather
seemed to be against them.
Slowly, they climbed the front
steps of the tree house.

Wearily, they plopped themselves
down on the sofa in the living room. It
seemed like the dark rain clouds outside
had followed them in and were hanging
over them.

"Whatever is the matter?" asked
Mama.

"Yes," said Papa. "You both look
like you are about to get a tooth
drilled."

Brother and Sister sighed.

"Oh, we had a rough day at school," said Brother. "I didn't make the school basketball team."

"And I didn't get a part in the school show," added Sister, putting her chin in her hands.

"Oh, dear!" said Papa, concerned. "What a shame!"

"How disappointing!" said Mama. "Didn't Coach Grizzmeyer or Teacher Jane give you anything to do at all?"

"Well," said Brother, "they did give us something to do. I'm the team manager."

"And I'm the stage manager," said Sister. "But I don't want to do that! I want to be in the show!"

"And I want to be on the team!" said Brother.

"Well," said Mama, "I guess not everybody can be a star."

"But don't you think I deserve to be in the show?" asked Sister.

"Of course you do!" said Mama, giving her a hug. "You're a wonderful singer!"

"And don't you think I deserve to be on the team?" asked Brother.

"Of course you do!" said Papa, patting him on the shoulder. "You're a terrific basketball player!"

"I guess nobody else thinks so," said Sister gloomily. "I guess nobody at Bear Country School thinks much of us at all!" She heaved an even bigger sigh.

"Well," said Mama, "it's not going to do us any good sitting around here feeling sorry for ourselves. I was just about to go outside to cut some flowers. It's getting chilly at night, and I want to get them in before there's a frost. Why don't we all go out for a little walk?

"But it's raining," protested Brother.

"The rain's stopped," said Papa, looking out the window. Sure enough, the clouds had lifted and the sun was peeking out.

Papa got Honey Bear into her stroller, and they all went outside. Mama stopped to cut some flowers at the back gate. They were very beautiful—big bright yellow, orange, pink, and violet blossoms. Birds were coming out after the rain and were singing in the trees. A big blue butterfly came sailing by and stopped to sip nectar from Mama's flowers. By now, the clouds had all rolled away and the golden sun was shining over the countryside.

"Look!" said Papa. "A rainbow!"

As the rays of the sun shone through the last drops of rain, a beautiful rainbow stretched right across the sky. "Wow!" said Brother. "It's so bright!"

"What makes a rainbow?" asked Sister in wonder.

"Well," said Papa, "you see ... the light from the sun shines through the raindrops and creates a prismatic thingy, which bounces around from the um ... uh ..."

Mama interrupted. "The rainbow is a gift from God. It's a sign that the rain is past and the sun has come to warm the earth again. God puts the rainbow in the sky as a beautiful sign of his love for all the earth and all the creatures that he has made."

"Even us?" asked Brother.

"Of course!" said Papa. "God loves everybody!"

"What about wasps?" asked Sister. A wasp had stung her in the school yard a few days ago, and she was very afraid of them.

"Well … yes," said Papa, shooing one away that was buzzing around Mama's flowers. "God loves all his creation!"

"Does he love us even when we're bad?" wondered Brother, a little puzzled.

"Well ..." said Papa.

"What about when we're really, really bad?" asked Sister. "Like when Brother and I got into a fight and wouldn't speak to each other for a week?"

"Um ..." said Papa.

"Or that time Too-Tall Grizzly and his gang dared me to steal Farmer Ben's watermelon?" asked Brother.

"Uh ..." said Papa.

"Or when we watch too much TV?" put in Sister. "Or when I bite my nails? Or when we don't do our homework? Or when—"

"YES!" Mama broke in, suddenly. "He does!"

They all looked at her in surprise.

"You see," she explained patiently, "God wants us to be good. But he doesn't love us because we're good or bad. God loves us because he made us. It's a little bit like how mothers and fathers love their children."

"Oh," said Sister. "Like how you still love us even when we do things we're not supposed to?"

"That's right," said Papa. "Of course, we're disappointed when you misbehave. But we still love you! We even love you when you don't make the basketball team or get a part in the school show! And we're proud of you because your coach and teacher trusted you to be managers—special jobs for the most responsible cubs."

Brother and Sister smiled. They were beginning to feel slightly better about that little problem.

By now they had made their way down the lane to a spot
that overlooked Farmer Ben's farm. It was a lovely scene.
The cows were coming in from the pasture, the ducks were
swimming in the pond, bees were buzzing around their hives,
and the sun was setting behind the trees.

As the sky grew darker, they noticed a tiny point of light in the western sky.

"What's that?" wondered Brother.

"That's the evening star," said Papa. "It comes out just after sunset."

"Is that another sign of God's love?" asked Sister.

"Yes, dear," said Mama, giving her a hug. "It surely is!"

And, hand in hand, the Bear family turned for home and their evening meal.

The Berenstain Bears.
Faithful Friends

written by Jan and Mike Berenstain

 Living Lights™

 ZONDERkidz

Lizzy Bruin was Sister Bear's very best friend. It seemed like they had been best friends for a very long time.

Lizzy Bruin and Sister Bear had been through a lot together. Once they had a slumber party that got a little out of hand.

They were in the school play that time Brother forgot his lines.

They built their own clubhouse when Brother kept them out of his.

They played dress up
and dolls, and rode their
bikes, and picked flowers,
and rolled down hills, and
giggled.

Sister was glad she had such a good friend. She could always rely on Lizzy to be there for her. They hardly ever fought or argued. Not, that is, until Sister started to spend more time with Suzy MacGrizzie.

Suzy was a new cub in town. At first, Sister and her friends didn't pay much attention to Suzy. But then, Sister noticed how lonely Suzy was and invited her to play. From then on, Suzy was part of Sister's little group.

All of Sister's friends, including Lizzy, liked Suzy. She was one more cub to spend time with and enjoy.

But Suzy was a little different from the other cubs. For one thing, she read an awful lot. And she was interested in different things—science, for instance. Suzy invited Sister over one night to look at the sky. Suzy pointed her telescope up at the moon.

"Wow!" said Sister, looking into the eyepiece. "It looks so close." She could actually see mountains and valleys and craters on the moon. It was very interesting.

One day, Suzy asked Sister to go on a butterfly hunt with her. They took butterfly nets and went out into the fields.

Sister caught a big yellow butterfly with black stripes. Suzy caught one that had bright red and blue spots on it and long swallowtails. It was very beautiful. After they studied the butterflies for a while, they let them go, and the butterflies sailed up into the sky over the trees.

"They're so pretty!" said Sister.

On their way back, Suzy and Sister ran into Lizzy and their friends Anna and Millie. They were all carrying their Bearbie dolls. "Hiya, gang!" called Sister when she saw them. "Suzy and I were out catching butterflies. You should have seen the big yellow one I got!"

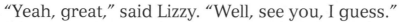

"Yeah, great," said Lizzy. "Well, see you, I guess."
"Wait a minute," said Sister. "Where are you all going?"
"We're going over to my garage to play Bearbie dolls," said Lizzy.
"Can Suzy and I come too?" asked Sister.

"It looks like you two are already pretty busy," said Lizzy. "Come on, girls." With that, Lizzy and her friends went on their way.

"How do you like that?" said Sister, hurt and angry. "Who does she think she is? Come on, Suzy, we'll play over at my house. Who needs them, anyway?"

When they got to the Bear family's tree house, Suzy and Sister found Brother Bear and Cousin Fred getting out their fishing tackle.

"Lizzy and your friends were here looking for you," Brother said. "I told them you were playing with Suzy. Lizzy didn't seem very happy."

"That Lizzy Bruin!" said Sister, annoyed. "What business is it of hers who I play with?"

"I guess she's jealous," said Brother.

"Jealous?" said Sister, puzzled.

"Sure," said Brother. "She's been your best friend for years. You mean a lot to her. She's just worried that maybe you don't like her as much as you used to."

"Oh," said Sister, "that's silly!" It was true that she liked her new friend, Suzy. But Lizzy would always be her best friend.

"What should I do?" Sister wondered.

Cousin Fred spoke up. "You know what the Bible says: 'Wounds from a friend can be trusted.'" Fred liked to memorize things.

"Huh?" said both Sister and Brother. "What does that mean?"

Suzy answered—she liked to memorize things too. "I think it means that when a friend who loves you hurts your feelings, you need to find out what is bothering her."

"Yes," Fred nodded. "And the Bible also says that we shouldn't stay angry with our friends. God wants us to make up with them if we have an argument."

"Oh," said Sister, thoughtfully.

"I have an idea," said Brother. "Fred and I were about to go fishing. Why don't we grab some extra fishing gear and go over to Lizzy's? We can see if they would all like to go fishing with us."

"Great!" said Sister. Suzy grinned.

So they all stopped by Lizzy's garage on their way to the fishing hole.

"Hey, Lizzy!" called Sister. "Do you and Anna and Millie want to go fishing with us?"

Lizzy acted like she wasn't so sure. But Anna and Millie were all for it, and Lizzy certainly didn't want to be left out.

Soon, they were all down at the fishing hole. Lizzy cast her line out into the middle of the pond and got her line into a terrible tangle.

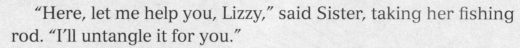

"Here, let me help you, Lizzy," said Sister, taking her fishing rod. "I'll untangle it for you."

"Wow, thanks!" said Lizzy. "You're a real friend, Sister."

"I always have been and I always will be!" said Sister, giving Lizzy a hug.

And together they picked away at the tangled fishing line.

The Berenstain Bears and A Job Well Done

written by
Jan and Mike Berenstain

Living Lights™

ZONDERkidz

It was spring in Bear Country. And that meant that it was
spring cleaning and fix-up time at the Bear family's tree house.
Mama, Papa, Brother, Sister, and even Honey all had jobs to do.

Mama and Papa got right down to work. Mama hung up rugs on the line to beat the dirt out of them. Papa started to fix the broken railing on the front steps.

Brother and Sister had a job too. They were supposed to clean up the old playhouse in the backyard. Honey was going to help them.

They all got off to a good start. The sun was shining, and the air was fresh and clean. Birds were singing, and bright flowers were blooming in the garden.

Mama whacked at the rugs. Huge clouds of dirt flew out of them.

Papa's tools were everywhere. He knelt down to carve a piece of wood into the right shape for the railing.

Brother, Sister, and Honey had everything they needed for their job. They had brooms and brushes, cloths and mops, buckets of hot water and lots of soap. First, they were going to sweep out the inside of the playhouse.

"Uh-oh!" said Brother, looking inside the playhouse. "Spiders!"

Sister and Honey peeked inside. Sure enough, there were some big, hairy spiders sitting in their webs up in the corners of the playhouse. Brother, Sister, and Honey hated spiders!

"Yuck!" they all said.

"What should we do?" asked Sister.

"Let's not sweep out the inside," said Brother. "Let's scrub the outside. Maybe that will scare the spiders out."

That's what they did. Brother worked his way around the playhouse with his scrub brush, whistling while he worked.

"Hey, look!" he said when he got to the back. "We left some baseball stuff out here."

There was an old baseball, a bat, and a glove behind the playhouse.

Brother picked up the ball, tossed it in the air, and caught it. Sister picked up the bat and gave it a few swings.

"Pitch it in!" she said to Brother.

Brother wound up and tossed the ball to Sister. She swatted it across the lawn.

"Here, Honey," said Brother, giving her the glove. "You be the outfielder."

Honey toddled out into the lawn and sat down.

Meanwhile, back at the tree house, Mama and Papa were hard at work. Mama was nearly done with the rugs. She was absolutely covered with dirt.

Papa was nearly finished with the railing. He fastened the wood in place, then straightened up and stretched.

That's when Papa noticed
Honey sitting in the middle
of the lawn. He couldn't see
Brother or Sister. They were
behind the tree house.
"What is Honey
doing just sitting there?"
wondered Papa.

A baseball came sailing into sight and landed near Honey. She grabbed it and threw it back.

"Hmmm!" said Papa, rubbing his chin.

Papa walked around the tree house and saw Brother and Sister playing baseball. Their brooms, brushes, cloths, and mops were all lying on the ground.

Papa stood behind Brother and Sister.

"Baseball is a fine springtime activity," he said, "but so is spring cleaning!"

Brother and Sister spun around and hid the ball and bat behind their backs.

"Oh, hi, Papa!" they both grinned. "We were just taking a little break."

Papa looked into the very dirty playhouse.

"It looks like you've been taking a *big* break," he said. "You've hardly touched this playhouse."

"But Papa," started Brother.

"There are lots of spiders in there!" finished Sister.

Papa smiled. He remembered how scared he was of spiders when he was a cub. He still didn't like them very much. "Well," he said, "I'll chase the spiders out for you. But, then, you need to get the job done."

Papa chased the spiders out of the playhouse with a broom. They ran off and hid in the storage shed, which was a better home for them, anyway.

Then, Brother, Sister, and Honey went back to work.

"Did you know that the Bible has something to say about working hard and getting the job done?" asked Papa as they cleaned.

"No," said Brother.

"What does it say?" said Sister.

"It says," said Papa, "'finish your outdoor work and get your fields ready; after that, build your house.'"

"Did you build a house today, Papa?" asked Sister.
"Well," said Papa, proudly, "I built a new railing."
"And," added Mama, who had come up to see what was going on, "it says in the Bible that God made work for us to do and there's nothing better than to enjoy your work."

"Did you enjoy your work, Mama?" asked Brother.
Mama rubbed some of the dirt off her face. "Well," she said, "I
enjoy my clean rugs—and you will enjoy your clean playhouse."

"Especially without all those spiders!" agreed Sister.
"Yuck!" said Honey.
Mama, Papa, Brother, and Sister all laughed.

The Berenstain Bears AND THE GIFT OF COURAGE

written by Jan and Mike Berenstain

Living Lights™

ZONDERkidz

Sister loved all animals—not only dogs and cats and birds and bunnies, but lizards and frogs and worms and bugs as well. She knew they were all God's creatures, and she liked to play with them. That's what caused the trouble with Too-Tall.

Too-Tall Grizzly and his gang were the official bullies of Bear Country School. They thought it was fun to push other cubs around, and they had many nasty ways to have fun.

One of their favorites was to bump into a cub on purpose and then make him apologize for being so clumsy.

Of course, they teased anyone anytime about pretty much anything at all. That's what happened to Sister Bear one morning in the school yard.

Sister was standing in line, waiting for the school bell to ring, when a cute little ladybug landed right on her shoulder.

She held out her finger so the ladybug could crawl onto it, and she chanted a line from an old nursery rhyme.

"Ladybug, ladybug, fly away home!"

As she watched the ladybug whirr away, Sister heard a nasty voice behind her. It was Too-Tall Grizzly.

"Ladybug, ladybug!" mocked Too-Tall. "Does Sister Bear wuv her wittle wadybug fwends?" he said in a silly, baby-talk voice. The rest of his gang laughed, and quite a few other cubs standing in line laughed with them.

Sister felt so embarrassed she froze. She didn't know what to say or do. She just stood there. Then the school bell rang, and the line began to move. She never got a chance to say or do anything at all.

For the rest of the day, Sister Bear felt terrible. She wished she had stood up against that nasty Too-Tall. She kept thinking of things that she "should have" said. *Maybe*, she thought, *I was just plain scared*! She didn't like the idea of being scared.

By bedtime that evening, Sister had almost stopped worrying about the Too-Tall incident—*almost*. It was Papa Bear's turn to read a bedtime story.

"What will it be tonight?" asked Papa as Brother and Sister snuggled down in their bunk beds.

A thought came into Sister's head. "How about David and Goliath?" she suggested.

"Yes," agreed Brother, "that's a good story."

"All right," said Papa,
"David and Goliath it is." He
got the *Big Book of Bible Stories*
for the cubs down from the
bookshelf and settled in to read.

"Long ago in the Holy Land, there lived a young shepherd named David. It was his job to watch over his father's flock of sheep. He knew that God was with him, so he was not afraid of wolves or lions.

"When wolves came sneaking up to the flock, David drove them away with stones from his sling.

"In those days, a giant warrior named Goliath was threatening those who lived in the Holy Land. Goliath towered over all other warriors. No one was brave enough to fight him.

"David heard about Goliath, but David was not afraid. He knew that God was watching over him. So he took some stones and his sling and went out against Goliath.

"When Goliath saw David, he laughed because David was only a boy. He raised his great spear to throw it at David.

"But David quickly put a stone in his sling and swung it around and around his head.

"He let it fly, and it struck Goliath right in the middle of his forehead. Goliath fell to the ground with a crash that shook the earth.

"Little David had struck down the giant warrior! With God's help, David had shown great courage and saved the land from Goliath."

The story was done, and Papa tucked Brother and Sister into bed.

"David was very brave, wasn't he?" asked Brother as Papa kissed them good night.

"He had the bravest heart of all," nodded Papa. "You know what they say, 'Little David was small—but, *oh, my!*'"

"I don't think I'm brave enough to stand up to someone so much bigger than I am," said Sister. "I would probably be too scared to even move."

"I don't know about that," said Papa, turning out the light. "I think both of you can be quite brave when you need to be. And remember, God is watching over you just like David. That will give you courage."

Brother and Sister fell asleep dreaming about the bravery of young David.

The next morning, Brother and Sister set off for school bright and early.
As they strolled along the road, they heard laughing and shouting up ahead.
They rounded a bend and saw Too-Tall Grizzly and his gang.

"I wonder what they're up to," said Brother.

"No good, I'll bet," said Sister.

As they came closer, they saw
that the gang was throwing rocks up
into a tree.

"What's going on, Too-Tall?"
asked Brother.

"You're just in time for some fun!" Too-Tall laughed. "See that hornets' nest up there?" He pointed at a huge round nest hanging high in the tree. "We're going to knock it down and see what happens."

"Don't do that!" said Sister. "That nest is the hornets' home. If you knock it down, they'll have no place to live."

"Aaaw!" sneered Too-Tall. "Are those hornets more of your wittle buggy fwends? Why don't you 'fly away' and mind your own business?"

While the gang laughed, Too-Tall drew back his arm to hurl a big rock at the nest. But Sister grabbed onto his arm.

"Hey, you little squirt!" yelled Too-Tall. "Let go!"

The rest of the gang charged at Sister to pull her away, but Brother stepped right in front of them. He glared at them. They didn't like the look in his eyes but Brother didn't seem the least bit afraid. They all backed away.

Too-Tall swung Sister around and around like David with his sling. But Sister hung on for all she was worth. Finally, Too-Tall gave a great heave and broke Sister's grip. The rock flew out of his hand and sailed up into the tree. It smacked right into the hornets' nest and knocked it open. A big cloud of angry hornets flew out.

Brother and Sister ducked under some bushes. The hornets bunched themselves up into an angry black ball and headed down after Too-Tall and his gang.

"Yeow!" yelled Too-Tall. "Look out!"

"Run!" yelled the gang.

When they were gone, Brother and Sister peeked out from behind the tree.

"That was close!" said Brother.

"Do you think God was watching over us?" wondered Sister.

"No doubt about it!" nodded Brother. With a sigh of relief, they continued on their way to school.

"You were very brave," said Brother, "going after Too-Tall that way. 'Little

Sister was small—but, *oh my!*'"

Sister laughed. "You were pretty brave yourself, standing up to the whole gang that way."

"I guess Papa was right," said Brother. "Even young cubs like us can be brave when we need to be."

"Too-Tall wasn't very brave," said Sister.

"Let's be fair," said Brother. "No one is very brave when it comes to angry hornets."

"No doubt about it!" agreed Sister,
and they walked on to school, arm in arm.

The Berenstain Bears® and the Trouble with THINGS

Activities and Questions from Brother and Sister Bear

Talk about it:

1. Brother and Sister have a lot of things. Do you have a lot of things? Which ones are the most important to you? How did you decide that? How would you feel if you did not have all of your things?

2. What has God given you? What is your most precious gift from God?

Get out and do it:

1. There are people who have very little. Talk with your family about how you can help someone in your church or community that is less fortunate than you. Work together as a family and do one of the following: have a canned food drive, collect blankets in the winter for the homeless, get others to participate and have a bake sale. Give the proceeds to the poor.

2. Say thank you to God! As a family, pray together, thanking God for all of the gifts he has given you. Thanking him is not only for Thanksgiving time, but for all the time!

The Berenstain Bears®

Gossip Gang

Activities and Questions from Brother and Sister Bear

Talk about it:

1. Have you ever heard someone gossiping or talking about someone else? Have you ever gossiped about someone else? How did that make you feel?

2. What made Sister uncomfortable when she thought about what she had said about her friend Anna?

3. Why is gossiping wrong? If you have some news about someone that you would like to talk about, what are some options besides gossip?

4. Is it ever OK to talk about other people?

Get out and do it:

1. Be positive! Be careful what you say about others. Cut out about 20 construction-paper bees and cover a jar with brown paper to look like a hive. For one week, every time you feel like talking about someone in a gossipy way, take a bee, write a good thing about that person on it, and place it in the jar!

2. As a family, talk about someone that needs your prayers and good thoughts ... that is a good kind of "talking about someone." Then, as a family, pray together for that person, asking for God to guide and bless him.

The Berenstain Bears®

Show Some Respect

Activities and Questions from Brother and Sister Bear

Talk about it:

1. What does "respect others" mean? To whom should we show respect? Do we only have to show respect to those older than we are?

2. Have you ever felt that someone did not give you respect that you deserved? How did that make you feel? Did you talk about it with that person?

3. Which of God's Ten Commandments talk about respect? Explain.

Get out and do it:

Show respect to people in your community. There are many ways!

a) Make cards for the elderly or sick in your church family and take them to the hospital or nursing home.
b) Organize a group of friends to rake leaves, cut grass, or do yard clean-up for people in your neighborhood.
c) Organize a food drive or blanket collection for those in your larger community that are less fortunate than you. Deliver the items to a local shelter or take to your church for distribution.

The Berenstain Bears®
Kindness Counts

Activities and Questions from Brother and Sister Bear

Talk about it:

1. Do you have a special talent or hobby? How did you first become interested in this hobby? How did Brother become interested in model airplanes?

2. Why did Brother hesitate before actually sharing his model airplane with Billy? Why is it sometimes difficult to share something you really like and other times very easy?

3. Describe a time that you have shown kindness to someone and been shown a kindness in return. Do you think that you need to be rewarded every time you do something nice? Why or why not?

Get out and do it:

1. Create a poster for your family to hang in a prominent place in the house. Have the following scripture phrase on it: "In everything, do to others what you would want them to do to you." (Matthew 7:12)

2. Organize a family hobby day. Have each family member share what they enjoy doing the most with the rest of the family. Remember to be kind as you explain directions and show others your hobby.

The Berenstain Bears

God Loves You!

Activities and Questions from Brother and Sister Bear

Talk about it:

1. Why did the director and coach choose Brother and Sister as managers instead of for the parts they wanted?

2. What are some signs of God's love around you right now?

Get out and do it:

1. Draw or paint a beautiful rainbow, flower, or butterfly.

2. Make a photo album of people you love. Add cutouts, stickers, and drawings of hearts, rainbows, and stars to remind you that signs of God's love are everywhere.

3. Count how many times you can bounce a ball without stopping. Try bouncing it different ways and count (with a clap in between, with your other hand, between your legs, etc.).

The Berenstain Bears®
Faithful Friends

Activities and Questions from Brother and Sister Bear

Talk about it:

1. How can you invite new friends into your friend group?

2. Have you ever felt left out by a friend? What do you think God would want you to do when that happens?

3. Do you like to do different things with different friends? Name some things you do differently.

Get out and do it:

1. Design a constellation—a group of stars that make a picture. Tape a piece of black paper over the end of an empty toilet paper tube. Use a pin to poke holes in the paper in a design. Look through the tube at a light to see your constellation design.

2. Draw a fish outline. Fill the outline with crayon textures, cut paper, and other materials to create eyes, mouth, and textured scales and fins.

3. Play Follow the Leader. Take turns being the leader.

The Berenstain Bears.

and A Job Well Done

Activities and Questions from Brother and Sister Bear

Talk about it:

1. Do you have at-home jobs that need to get done before you can have some fun? Name some of the chores you do and how it helps the family when you finish them completely.

2. What do you think Papa Bear meant when he said the Bible says, "finish your outdoor work and get your fields ready; after that, build your house?"

Get out and do it:

1. Design a family chore chart. Hang the chart up and check it daily, making sure you are completing your family responsibilities.

2. Help someone in your family with one of their given jobs around the house. Do not wait to be asked!

The Berenstain Bears®
AND THE GIFT OF COURAGE

Activities and Questions from Brother and Sister Bear

Talk about it:

1. What does it mean to be a bully?

2. Have you ever had to stand up to someone who is a bully? What would God want you to do if you met a bully?

3. How can you be brave when you meet someone who is not so nice?

Get out and do it:

1. Draw two barbells on heavy paper or cardboard and cut them out. Write the following words on the barbells and then hang them up in your room to remind you how to act when you feel threatened: Strong at Heart, Strong in Mind.

2. Design a card to give to someone who you believe is brave. It can be for a friend, your mom or dad, or a neighbor. Tell that person how much you admire his courage. Thank the person for showing you how to be courageous like David!

The Berenstain Bears®

Living Lights™

9780310712503
$3.99

9780310712497
$3.99

9780310712527
$3.99

9780310712565
$3.99

9780310720898
$3.99

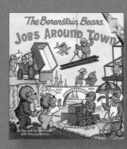
9780310722861
$3.99

9780310720904
$3.99

A Lift the Flap Book
9780310720812
$6.99

A Lift the Flap Book
9780310720836
$6.99

Stickers Included
9780310720850
$4.99

Stickers Included
9780310720881
$4.99

ZONDERkidz™
.com

The Berenstain Bears®

Living Lights™

Bind-ups

5 Books in 1
9780310720102
$10.99

5 Books in 1
9780310725916
$10.99

3 Books in 1
9780310734925
$7.99

3 Books in 1
9780310735038
$7.99

Hardcover Titles

9780310719366
$6.99

9780310719373
$6.99

9780310719380
$6.99

9780310719397
$6.99

9780310722762
$6.99

9780310727149
$6.99

9780310722779
$6.99

9780310727132
$6.99

ZONDERkidz™
.com

The Berenstain Bears®

 **I Can Read!™** BEGINNING 1 READING

3 Books in 1
9780310734178
$9.99

9780310725015
$3.99

9780310725091
$3.99

9780310720973
$3.99

9780310720980
$3.99

9780310721000
$3.99

9780310720997
$3.99

9780310721024
$3.99

9780310721017
$3.99

ZONDERkidz™
.com

The Berenstain Bears®

Living Lights™

Storybook Bible

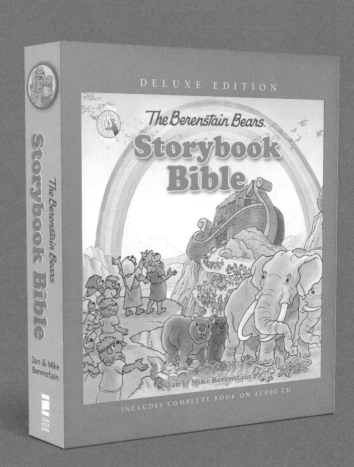

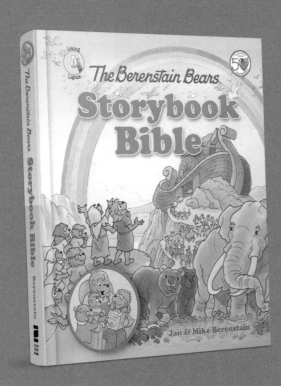

9780310727217
$16.99

Audio included
9780310742241
$24.99